Scholastic Canada Ltd.
604 King Street West, Toronto, Ontario M5V 1E1, Canada

Scholastic Inc.
557 Broadway, New York, NY 10012, USA

Scholastic Australia Pty Limited
PO Box 579, Gosford, NSW 2250, Australia

Scholastic New Zealand Limited
Private Bag 94407, Botany, Manukau 2163, New Zealand

Scholastic Children's Books
Euston House, 24 Eversholt Street, London NW1 1DB, UK

www.scholastic.ca

Library and Archives Canada Cataloguing in Publication
Larry, H. I., author
Thrill ride / H.I. Larry ; illustrated by Andy Hook.
(Zac Power)
Previously published: Richmond, Victoria : Hardie Grant
Egmont, 2012.
ISBN 978-1-4431-4635-7 (paperback)
I. Hook, Andy, illustrator II. Title. III. Series: Larry,
H. I. Zac Power.
PZ7.L333Th 2016   j823'.92   C2015-904757-9

Published in Australia by Hardie Grant Egmont, 2009.
First Canadian edition published 2016.
Cover design and illustrations by Andy Hook.
Typeset by Ektavo.

6 5 4 3 2 1   Printed in Canada 121   16 17 18 19 20

MIX
Paper from
responsible sources
FSC® C004071

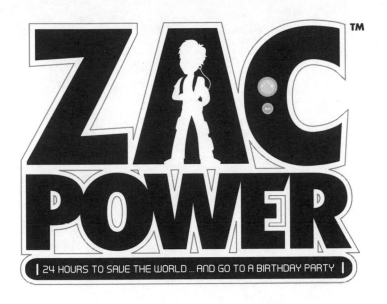

ZAC POWER™

24 HOURS TO SAVE THE WORLD ... AND GO TO A BIRTHDAY PARTY

THRILL RIDE

BY *H. I. LARRY*

ILLUSTRATIONS BY *ANDY HOOK*

Scholastic Canada Ltd.
Toronto New York London Auckland Sydney
Mexico City New Delhi Hong Kong Buenos Aires

CHAPTER...
...ONE

"WHY'S THE MUSIC SO LOUD?" yelled Leon, jamming his fingers in his ears.

Zac Power and his brother Leon were front row at the Axe Grinder concert. Axe Grinder was Zac's favourite band.

"Sounds like a cat with its tail jammed in a door!" whined Leon, but Zac could hardly hear him above the music.

If only Zac's mum hadn't made Leon come to the concert, too…

"AXE GRINDER ROCKS!" Zac yelled.

Zac didn't normally have time to do stuff like this. Although he was only twelve, he worked as a top-secret spy for GIB (or Government Investigation Bureau). Missions and training kept him super busy.

Last holiday, he'd spent two entire weeks doing GIB's Fear Management course. Not that he had any fear to start with! His mum and dad were GIB spies, too. Fearlessness was in his blood.

Even Leon's not afraid…of being too geeky, Zac thought, laughing to himself.

Leon worked for GIB Tech Support. He designed gadgets and operated GIB's supercomputers. Leon's code name was Agent Tech Head.

The chorus of Axe Grinder's latest hit was playing. Zac was singing at the top of his lungs, rocking out. He strummed his air guitar wildly.

Then someone tapped him on the back.

What kind of moron would interrupt Axe Grinder's best song? fumed Zac, turning around.

It was Angus Poulter from school. He was eight and thought Zac was really cool. Angus didn't know Zac was a spy – that was top secret. But Angus copied Zac's hairstyles and backpack anyway. He even wanted to change his name to Zac!

"Are…are you…here by yourself?" Angus stammered.

Zac pointed at Leon and shook his head.

"I brought my mum," said Angus.

A woman in a pink track suit waved at them. Angus blushed.

Angus makes Leon look cool! Zac thought. *And that's saying something.*

"Do you…would you…" Angus began.

Suddenly, Zac felt sorry for Angus. He couldn't help being shy.

"Wanna come to my ninth birthday

party tomorrow?" Angus blurted. "It's at twelve o'clock."

"Er…OK," said Zac, not knowing what else to say.

He'd be by far the oldest at Angus's party. Imagine if he had to play musical chairs! But there was no way out now. If Zac didn't show up, Angus would be crushed.

"Great, see ya!" said Angus, smiling happily. The huge crowd swallowed up Angus and his mum. In fact, the crowd was cheering and going crazier than ever.

What's going on? Zac wondered. Then he noticed an Axe Grinder fan. The kid was standing on the barrier in front of the stage. He was about to jump! Zac watched as he dived and was caught by the crowd below him.

Awesome! Zac thought. He had always wanted to stage-dive.

Zac elbowed through the crowd and jumped onto the barrier. In front of him, the crowd was a sea of faces and waving arms. The floor looked a long way down...

The crowd chanted,

"JUMP! JUMP! JUMP!"

What if they don't catch me? Zac worried for a moment. But he quickly squashed that thought. *A spy feels no fear!*

He took a deep breath and...

"WOOO-HOOOO!" Zac yelled,

sailing through the air. For a moment, he was flying!

Then Zac noticed a burly man dressed all in black pushing through the crowd, as if in slow motion. He looked like a typical bouncer.

He's standing right where I'm going to land! thought Zac, hurtling toward the man. *And he's shoving everyone out of the way!*

"You're coming with me," the man barked, catching Zac before he hit the floor.

"Easy, Meat Head," Zac muttered. "I know stage-diving's against the rules. But there's no need to chuck me out."

Gripping Zac tightly with his meaty

hands, the man dragged Zac through the crowd toward the exit door. Zac couldn't escape. The man was practically carrying him.

Zac looked at the man's T-shirt.

The bouncers have all got CROWD CONTROL printed on their T-shirts, Zac realized. *But this man's T-shirt is blank. He's not a real bouncer!*

Zac kicked and struggled. But the fake bouncer held on tight. He dragged Zac all the way around to the back of the stadium.

Zac had no idea what was about to happen. Then he caught sight of a silver bus with monster-truck wheels, parked just behind the stadium.

Huh? Zac thought. *That looks like Axe Grinder's tour bus!*

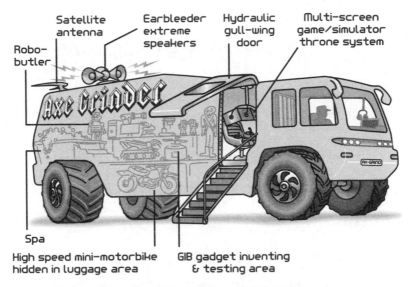

Satellite antenna

Earbleeder extreme speakers

Hydraulic gull-wing door

Multi-screen game/simulator throne system

Robo-butler

Spa

High speed mini-motorbike hidden in luggage area

GIB gadget inventing & testing area

GIB MOBILE TECHNOLOGY LAB
(Axe Grinder Tour Bus Disguise)

At last, the fake bouncer let go of Zac. "Agent Clawhammer, GIB Mission Control," he said, shaking Zac's hand. "We disguised the mission vehicle as a rock star's tour bus. Didn't want to stand out too much at the Axe Grinder concert."

"That's a cool bus," Zac admitted. "But why pretend to be a bouncer, Agent Clawhammer? I thought I was being kidnapped!"

Clawhammer coughed. "HQ believed leaving the Axe Grinder concert for a mission would…displease you."

They got that right, thought Zac grumpily, climbing aboard the bus.

CHAPTER... ...TWO

The features on the mission vehicle were awesome. Unlimited snacks. A library of all the latest movies on Blu-ray. Plus a full-sized spa to watch them in!

Before Zac could enjoy any of it, Agent Clawhammer handed him a mission disk. Zac put it into his SpyPad, the mini-computer all GIB spies carried.

CLASSIFIED

MISSION INITIATED: 12:04 P.M.

GIB has learned that BIG is holding its annual conference at Shark Park 24 hours from now.

Shark Park is a new 24-hour theme park on the north coast. It is home to the world's scariest roller coaster, the White Pointer.

YOUR MISSION:

A simple intelligence-gathering operation: bug the conference facility, disguising yourself as Captain Tentacles the Happy Octopus.

Remember, BIG agents have already begun arriving at Shark Park, so trust no one.

THRILL RIDE
>>> ON

Clawhammer gave Zac the Captain Tentacles costume.

"No way am I wearing this!" moaned Zac.

The costume was fluffy and pink with googly eyes. There was a sea-captain's hat and arms everywhere!

Clawhammer stifled a smirk. "Orders are orders," he said crisply.

Zac slumped into a nearby seat. "Shark Park is ages away. Why can't I put it on when I get closer?"

"No, you need to learn how the suit works, and get used to it," said Clawhammer.

With Clawhammer's help, Zac struggled into the suit, scowling. He looked like a

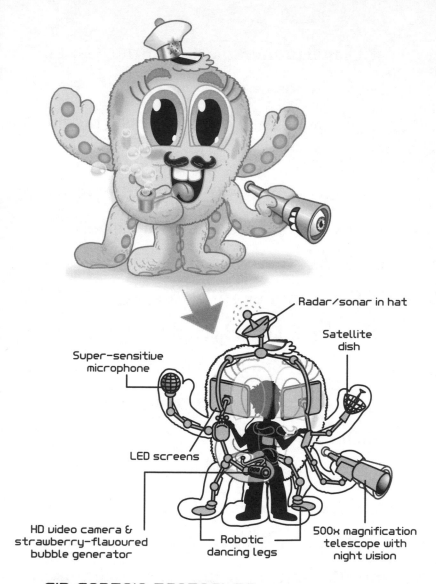

Radar/sonar in hat

Satellite dish

Super-sensitive microphone

LED screens

HD video camera & strawberry-flavoured bubble generator

Robotic dancing legs

500x magnification telescope with night vision

GIB CAPTAIN TENTACLES Surveillance Suit

giant pink marshmallow with legs!

"The first tentacle has a telescope," Clawhammer said, zipping Zac up. "There's a microphone for long-distance eavesdropping in another."

Clawhammer started the bus and they sped off. Zac tried out his suit, angling the satellite dish and zooming the telescope. When he got bored he tried playing Alien Attack on his SpyPad. But it was next to impossible with tentacles. The hours dragged by. At one point, Zac stretched out and had a nap. When he woke up, though, the bus wasn't even moving!

Zac glanced out the window. Cars were bumper-to-bumper for kilometres ahead.

That's why, thought Zac. *A monster traffic jam.* He checked his watch.

It was almost 5 p.m. *This is seriously uncool for a spy on a deadline,* Zac thought.

"Why didn't we take a chopper –" Zac began to ask Clawhammer. Then he noticed a lever on the dashboard.

The label read "High Speed Mini-Motorbike Release."

On a mini-motorbike, I'd be able to weave through the traffic, Zac thought. He decided to take charge.

"Time for Plan B. Turn off there," Zac told Clawhammer, pointing to a freeway exit.

Clawhammer pulled out of the traffic. Then, when he was sure they were alone, Zac hit the motorbike release lever.

"Unzip the octopus suit!" Zac yelled to Clawhammer.

"No can do, Agent Rock Star," said Clawhammer. "You need help to put that costume on or take it off, and you'll be on your own at Shark Park."

I can't believe I've got to ride to Shark Park dressed like this, Zac thought. *That's not only mega-embarrassing, it's bad spying.*

It's hard to snoop around in an octopus suit!

Grabbing some basic gadgets from the bus, Zac jumped off and walked around the side. A hydraulic arm was lowering the motorbike out of the bus's luggage-storage compartment.

Zac inspected the shining chrome engine. He couldn't wait to jump on.

Zac engaged the GPS Mode on his SpyPad. An alternative route via the back roads popped up on the screen.

It'll still take me a while to get to Shark Park this way, thought Zac. *But it's better than that traffic jam.*

Zac swung his tentacles over the bike. He started the bike, and the engine growled.

He was off! Zac sped along the dusty back roads, completely alone. He saw a huge rock and decided to have some fun. The bike soared skyward over the rock. *Way cooler than a traffic jam!* he thought, landing with a bump and roaring off.

As minutes turned into hours, Zac consulted his GPS. He was close to Shark Park now.

Then the fuel gauge caught his eye. Zac had ridden so far out of his way, the tank was nearly empty.

Heading down the highway, Zac found a gas station and pulled in.

Phew, thought Zac. *There's no one around.*

Except...

A red-headed man was filling up cans with gasoline. He was having trouble working the gas pump, though.

Odd, thought Zac. *You don't have to be a genius to work a gas pump…*

Zac rode up next to him, and the man looked up suddenly.

Zac took in every detail about the man, right down to his silver SkatePro X1s. *He might not be smart,* Zac thought, *but he's got wicked taste in sneakers!*

The man gave Zac a big, fake smile. "What's an octopus doing on a motorbike?" he asked slowly.

Zac had to think quickly.

CHAPTER ... THREE

There was no way Zac was giving anything away to the red-headed man. He could be a BIG agent on his way to the conference!

Although he seems a bit thick, Zac thought. Zac didn't like to give BIG agents too much credit, but they were usually pretty smart.

"I'm on my way to work," Zac said

confidently. "At Shark Pa—"

But the man cut him off. "Shark Park?" The man was so worked up, he showered spit on Zac's octopus costume.

He's very interested in Shark Park, Zac thought. *Maybe he is BIG after all.*

"Yup," said Zac. "Heard of it?"

"Er, no," said the man. "Why would I?"

Zac glanced down the highway. You could easily see Shark Park's neon lights from the gas station.

"I mean, yes," said the man. "Course I've heard of it. Do you think I'm stupid?"

Something's off about this guy, Zac thought, his spy senses tingling.

"So, anyway…how did you get the job

at Shark Park?" the man asked casually.

Zac checked the time.

Gotta give this guy the slip, Zac thought. The ride had taken ages. Zac was running out of time before the conference started, and he still needed time to look around.

Zac jingled the bike keys in his hand. Leon's latest invention, the HypnoTick, was attached.

The HypnoTick looked like a key ring. But when Zac pressed a button on the side, the chain started moving. It swung back and forth. Anyone who saw it was instantly hypnotized for thirty minutes.

It's rude to hypnotize strangers, Zac thought. *But a spy's got to do what a spy's got to do.*

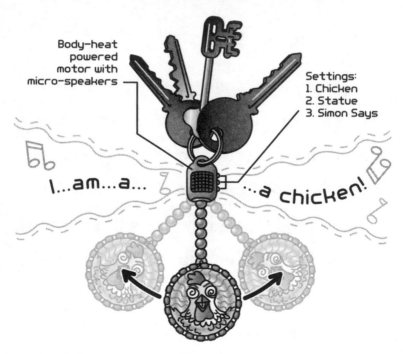

Body-heat powered motor with micro-speakers

Settings:
1. Chicken
2. Statue
3. Simon Says

I...am...a...

...a chicken!

GIB HYPNOTICK Instant Hypnotism Keychain

Zac set the HypnoTick to "Chicken." He pointed the HypnoTick at the man.

A second later...

BRRRR-RRRRRRRRRUK! BRUK! BRUK!

The man flapped his arms like wings. He even clucked like a chicken!

Zac laughed so hard his stomach hurt.

Wish I could stay and watch, Zac grinned to himself. *But I've got to get to Shark Park — now!*

Zac rode flat out toward Shark Park's front gate. You couldn't miss it — it was a giant, glowing face with huge shark teeth jutting from the mouth.

Zac stopped nearby and watched how the gate worked. The mouth opened. Kids and parents ran through. Then… **SNAP!** The mouth closed. Someone's mum got her jacket caught on a shark tooth. She looked terrified.

If Shark Park's gates are this scary, Zac thought, *what's the rest of the park going to be like?*

Zac could see the conference centre from the gate, but there were people everywhere.

Any one of those people could be a BIG spy, he thought.

Zac didn't want to go in the front gates. Everyone would see him if he did. So he circled Shark Park's razor-wire fence on his motorbike. He could see all kinds of shark-themed rides from over the fence.

Right away, Zac spotted the White Pointer roller coaster, looping and plummeting. Even from far away he could hear kids screaming.

Well, it is the world's scariest roller coaster, he thought.

Zac heard more screams, coming from the Tiger Shark this time. That was a giant shark-shaped carriage that swung into the air and went round a full 360 degrees.

Zac could also see the Ghost Shark's Haunted Ship, inside a huge building. There was even a World of Sharks aquarium.

Cool, thought Zac. *I bet they've got all the super-dangerous sharks in there.*

Then Zac spotted a garbage dump. There was a gap in the fence. He could sneak into Shark Park!

Zac killed the bike's engine and stashed the bike in some nearby bushes. He began to crawl through the gap in the fence. His tentacles kept getting tangled in the wire.

Forget orders, he thought. *I'm never dressing like fluffy pink sea-life again!*

But at last he made it through.

Empty cardboard boxes were stacked everywhere.

"Ice cream cones," read the nearest box. "Plastic shark fins," said another.

Guess they sell them at the souvenir shops, Zac thought.

A third box was labelled "telescopic gunsights." *What would a theme park need with gun parts?* Zac wondered. *Or are they for toy guns? Or for BIG?*

Zac had lots of questions. One stood out above the rest. *Would BIG be dumb enough to leave such a gigantic clue lying around?*

Just then, Shark Park's PA system crackled to life. "ATTENTION, CAPTAIN TENTACLES THE HAPPY OCTOPUS. REPORT IMMEDIATELY TO THE SECURITY OFFICE."

Captain Tentacles? Security office? That did *not* sound good.

CHAPTER... ...FOUR

Zac hid behind an empty box. He needed to think. *Security's after Captain Tentacles! Does BIG know I'm here?* Zac wondered.

It didn't make sense. BIG were only supposed to be having a conference at Shark Park. *But somehow they've got control of security!* Zac thought. He thought of the gunsights box with a sinking feeling.

This mission seems much bigger than GIB realizes, Zac decided, gritting his teeth.

And somehow, he had blown his cover already. *How did they get onto me so fast?* he thought. *They must have cameras everywhere, even at the garbage dump!*

But then something else occurred to him. The red-headed man at the gas station was the only one who knew that Captain Tentacles was heading to Shark Park. *And the timing fits,* Zac thought, glancing at his watch.

The HypnoTick would've worn off 13 minutes ago, giving the red-headed man time to get here. Maybe he works for BIG. They're planning something evil at their conference, and he thinks I'm trying to stop them, Zac thought. Although the man had seemed a bit…well…thick to work for BIG.

One thing was certain. Security was searching Shark Park for a pink octopus. *If I can get rid of the suit,* Zac realized, *I'll look like an ordinary kid.*

But the suit would be hard to get off. And Zac needed somewhere secure to get changed.

The garbage dump was hidden from the rest of Shark Park by a brick wall. A door in the wall stood slightly ajar.

Perfect, thought Zac. *A storeroom.*

He went inside and shut the door behind him. The lock clicked softly. Zac looked around.

Uh-oh.

Zac wasn't in a storeroom. He'd walked through a back door into one of Shark Park's most famous attractions: the World of Sharks aquarium!

WORLD

'SUB SHARK'
NEWLY DISCOVERED SPECIES
WARNING! – EXTREMELY
DANGEROUS!   KEEP CLEAR!

of SHARKs

The World of Sharks building was huge. There were lots of tanks, each with a different breed of shark inside.

Zac recognized most of them right away. There was the hammerhead, a weird grey shark with a head like a double-ended hammer. There were harmless little reef sharks. And Zac's personal favourite – a pair of crazy makos ready to eat you whole.

The set-up was impressive. Water flowed through underground pipes that joined the tanks with the open sea, so the sharks always had salt water.

The World of Sharks was packed! Every kid there wanted to check out the sharks.

The kids will just think I'm one of Shark

Park's mascots, Zac thought. *But what if security sees me? Or a BIG agent? Or are they the same thing?*

Zac crept toward the shadows. A massive 3-D model of undersea life lined one wall of the aquarium. It was like the displays Zac had seen in museums on boring school excursions.

Zac snuck into an empty spot beside a life-sized killer whale model and froze in place. At the last minute, he remembered to rip off his sea-captain's hat. Without it, Captain Tentacles looked like part of the display. If you didn't look too hard...

Keeping his head still, Zac scanned the room with his telescopic tentacle. He

focused on one of the World of Sharks'
signs.

The sign said "Sub Shark." *But I've never
heard of them,* Zac thought. *And I know every
shark species alive.*

Zac looked closer at the tank under the
sign.

*Those sub sharks look ten metres long! Even
a white pointer's only six metres.*

Then Zac heard something. Footsteps...
and they were coming his way!

"Ginger here. Do you read me, over?"
a woman said.

Zac was dying to see who this Ginger
was. But he couldn't — if he moved, he'd
give away his hiding spot!

Luckily, the ultra-sensitive microphone in Zac's other tentacle was on. He heard a man's voice through Ginger's earpiece. It was garbled, but Zac made out most of it.

"Sorry, Ginger..." the man said. "*SSkhhhkshs*...suspicious...Captain Tentacles...*sshhshs* hypnotized...got away...now worried...compromised the mission...Over."

That sounds like the man from the gas station, Zac thought.

"Don't worry about it, Dwayne," Ginger said. "Don't let what happened with BIG ruin your confidence."

BIG? Zac thought. *What happened with BIG?*

"You would have made a great agent," Ginger was saying. "And you haven't compromised our mission. Testing is nearly complete. Operation White Pointer is still on track."

"Thanks. Any sign of Captain Tentacles?" came the man's reply.

Zac held his breath. What was BIG up to this time? And who were Ginger and Dwayne? Whatever was going on, it sounded like every single person at Shark Park was at risk. It was up to Zac to save them.

And Ginger might spot him at any second!

CHAPTER... ...FIVE

"Negative, Dwayne," said Ginger. "Captain Tentacles is not — I repeat, NOT — in the World of Sharks."

She walked off. Relief flooded through Zac.

Then there was another announcement over the PA. "FEEDING IS COMMENCING AT THE MAKOS' TANK."

The makos were way over on the other side of the exhibition. The crowd rushed toward their tank.

Alone now, Zac seized his chance. He remembered Clawhammer saying you needed two people to take the suit off. It was difficult, but Zac unzipped the octopus suit a few centimetres. He grabbed the penknife that hung from a cord around his neck. He sliced the suit down the front. Once he'd got it off, Zac hurled the suit into a shark tank. The sharks ripped it to shreds in seconds.

Good riddance, Captain Tentacles, he thought.

Zac was stiff from standing still for so

long. But at least he now had a lead on the mission.

Ginger and Dwayne are definitely involved in BIG's evil operation at Shark Park, Zac thought. *Operation White Pointer sounds like the code name.*

Zac wasn't exactly sure how a BIG plot could involve the world's scariest roller coaster. But he headed straight to the White Pointer to find out!

Outside, the sky was darkest black. Zac could hear kids screaming as the White Pointer ride whirled around in huge loops.

The White Pointer towered above the rest of the rides. The tallest roller coaster ever, it went from zero to 160 kilometres per hour in two seconds. It dropped 200 metres straight down!

For most people, the White Pointer would be incredibly scary. But as a top spy, Zac was fearless. If investigating Operation White Pointer meant riding the world's scariest roller coaster, so be it. *It's a tough job, but someone's gotta do it,* Zac thought.

He joined the massive ticket lineup. Although the White Pointer was strictly for kids over twelve, Zac noticed lots of much younger kids were lining up, too.

Maybe the ticket-sellers bend the rules, thought Zac. *They don't want anyone missing out, I guess.*

After waiting for ages, Zac reached the front of the line. He crossed a small platform and boarded the roller coaster. The White Pointer was made up of ten carriages joined together. Each carriage was shaped like a gaping shark's mouth.

Zac jumped into a carriage. A harness clamped across him. Blood pounded in his ears. The carriage lurched forward. The ride had begun!

What's all the fuss about? Zac thought as they started off quite slowly. *This isn't scary at —*

"…AAAAAAAAAHHHHHHHHHH!"

A scream tore through Zac's throat as the White Pointer plunged 200 metres straight down! Zac could hardly see straight.

The ground rushed up at him. Zac gripped his harness, white-knuckled. This ride was amazing!

Overhead, a camera flashed.

The carriage swung sideways. A second camera flashed. The White Pointer hurtled into a triple upside-down corkscrew. Zac counted another camera flash, and then another.

The White Pointer rocketed into an insane loop. Then it took the same loop at double speed – backwards! And before Zac knew what was happening, they shot into a pitch-black tunnel half-filled with water.

Suddenly, a White Pointer shark leaped from the murky water. Zac screamed again with excitement. A camera took another photo of him. The shark snapped its teeth, then disappeared.

Phew, thought Zac, noticing a mechanical

pole attached to the shark. *It's robotic!*

At last, the carriage shot out of the dark and glided to a stop. An older kid got off and threw up in a bin. Dads were quivering messes. Zac staggered across the platform, dazed but grinning.

Near the exit, Zac saw a souvenir stand with photos of the White Pointer ride. There were four different shots of his screaming face.

Four photos, thought Zac. *Didn't I count five flashes? There should be a photo of me when the shark jumped out…shouldn't there?*

Zac was suspicious. He checked his watch. Another White Pointer ride was due to start soon.

There's just time to sneak into the tunnel, scale the wall and check out what made the extra flash, Zac thought.

The attendants were busy taking tickets for the next ride. Zac crept into the dark tunnel and found himself knee-deep in water.

Climbing the tunnel wall to get to the cameras would be difficult. Luckily Zac had the perfect gadget – Gecko Gloves.

Gecko Gloves had ultra-sticky suction

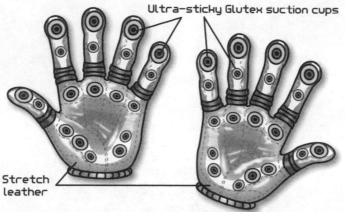

Ultra-sticky Glutex suction cups

Stretch leather

GIB GECKO GLOVES – Adhesive Climbing Gloves

cups on the fingertips. Slipping them on, Zac scaled the wall, clinging on by his fingertips like a gecko. The fifth camera was almost within reach when he heard something...

Footsteps were sloshing through the tunnel. Someone was coming. And they were coming fast!

CHAPTER... ...SIX

Zac's pulse was racing. He pushed the roof above him. A tile shifted, just in time. Zac squeezed through the gap and outside onto the roof of the tunnel. He moved the tile back into position, leaving a small crack to look through.

Zac could make out a shadowy figure in the tunnel below. The figure took down the camera with a special long pole. Then the figure opened the camera and took out a strange object.

Zac needed more information. He engaged his SpyPad's camera. He turned off the flash, so as not to give himself away, and snapped a photo just before the figure disappeared out of the tunnel.

Alone again, Zac climbed back down into the tunnel and snuck away.

Zac looked at the photo. It was almost black, as expected. Luckily, Leon had just written some new SpyPad software, called Photofix. The program fixed dark or grainy photos, pixel by pixel, until every detail was clear.

Switching on Photofix, Zac could see that the figure in the photo was definitely the red-headed man from the gas station! Zac was sure he was Dwayne. In the photo, Dwayne was holding what looked like an oversized battery, only clear. A smoky gas was trapped inside.

It looks like an energy cell, Zac thought.

Zac texted the photo to Leon. Using GIB's database of BIG agents, Leon would be able to find out about Dwayne. Any information would be useful.

Leon will be home in bed, Zac realized. *I'll follow Dwayne while I wait for Leon's reply.*

Zac grabbed his AquaReader from the gadget kit in his backpack. The AquaReader looked like a light. But it was designed to make water particles glow fluorescent.

Dwayne's SkatePro X1s would've got wet in the tunnel. The microscopic water particles left behind will still glow.

Zac switched on the AquaReader. There, right in front of him, were crisp, glowing SkatePro X1 prints.

The prints led Zac away from the White Pointer roller coaster. They snaked toward a deserted corner of Shark Park, turned a corner, then stopped.

Zac stood face to face with a curved wall made of wooden planks. At ground level, he noticed a small trap door.

Zac took his spy sunglasses from his backpack and engaged Night Vision Mode. His sharp spy vision spotted a hair. Even in the dark, the hair had a red tinge.

Dwayne definitely went this way, thought Zac, taking his sunglasses off. He looked pretty lame wearing sunglasses at night.

Zac pushed the trap door. He couldn't believe it. Dwayne had left it open!

Nice one, genius, Zac thought.

He crept through. Instantly, he was plunged into total darkness. Was Dwayne hiding somewhere in the gloom?

The air was deathly cold. Goosebumps sprang up on Zac's arms. He shivered.

This place is creepy.

"MMMMMMMMMPPHH!"

Zac muffled a scream. Something brushed his arm!

It felt like…

Zac's insides knotted.

…a skeleton!

Luckily GIB's Fear Management course had taught Zac to stay calm in scary situations.

There must be a rational explanation, Zac told himself. *What kind of skeleton would you find at a theme park?*

Zac thought of all of Shark Park's

attractions. Then he almost laughed with relief. *I'm in the Ghost Shark's Haunted Ship!*

The Ghost Shark ride was a giant fake ship. Visitors rode through in a carriage as scary shark skeletons jumped out.

I'm on the ground, Zac thought. *So the carriage tracks are above my head.*

Suddenly, Zac's SpyPad vibrated. A reply from Leon!

MESSAGE
RECEIVED 5:46 A.M.

Sorry, the GIB database has no information on Dwayne so I'd say he doesn't work for BIG.

The computer did find an old ID photo that LOOKS a lot like Dwayne, though. It's of Janet Wolfe. Weird, huh?

Janet Wolfe! Zac knew all the rumours. Once a top evil agent with BIG, Janet

Wolfe was famous for paralyzing people with a single press to the neck. Then one day, without warning or explanation, she left BIG. No one knew where she'd gone.

Zac paced up and down, thinking. How could Dwayne be involved in a BIG plot if he didn't work for them? And why did he look like Janet Wolfe?

In the gloom, Zac walked into a fake treasure chest. *Ouch!* He'd banged his knee. He took another step and – "AAAAAAH!" he screamed.

The treasure chest was moving! Underneath it was a big hole, and Zac was falling through it.

CHAPTER... ...SEVEN

Zac plummeted at top speed through the hole. His mind was racing.

That treasure chest must've been a hidden trap door! Zac thought, catching a glimpse as he fell. *And now it looks like I'm falling into an underground bunker.*

Zac was seconds away from smashing into the concrete floor when —

HSSSSSSSSSSS

His Safe-T-Shirt! It was fitted with front and rear airbags. Just in time, they suddenly inflated and cushioned his landing. It was like landing on a beanbag.

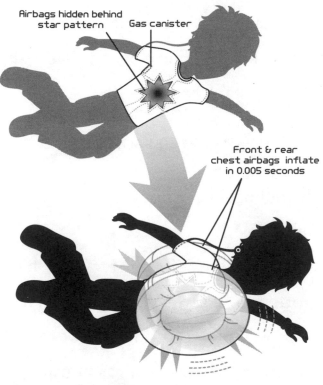

Airbags hidden behind star pattern

Gas canister

Front & rear chest airbags inflate in 0.005 seconds

GIB SAFE-T-SHIRT

Zac leaped to his feet and deflated his T-shirt. The bunker was deserted. One wall was totally covered with CCTV screens. Each screen showed a different part of Shark Park.

On a stainless steel bench sat a fish tank. Zac peered in. There was a baby shark inside! The tank was labelled:

FEAR ~~FAKTOR~~ FACTOR: 6/10

It looked like whoever wrote the sign couldn't spell.

Dwayne? he thought. Zac hadn't forgotten how Dwayne had carelessly left the Ghost Ship trap door unlocked. And he couldn't even work a gas pump! *I don't think he's the sharpest tool in the box…*

Next to the fish tank, Zac spotted some horror DVDs.

MY MUM WAS A BRAIN-EATING ZOMBIE FF: 2

KILLER SLUGS 2 - REVENGE OF THE SLIME FF: 5.7

There was a scale model of the White Pointer ride. A sign attached read: *FF: 9.9.*

Zac knew the ride was truly terrifying for normal people. He'd seen *Killer Slugs 2*, which was not that scary.

Someone's rated the fear factor of these things! Zac realized.

Was it Dwayne? And who was Ginger? At first Zac had thought that they worked for BIG. But Leon's message made him think otherwise.

If this place really is a secret bunker, thought Zac, *the answer could be here.*

Frantically, Zac searched the bunker. The BIG conference was only hours away, and Zac hadn't placed a single bug yet. But Ginger and Dwayne could be endangering everyone at Shark Park! He had to stop them before he could bug anything.

Finally, Zac discovered a small, high-tech machine hidden under a cover.

The top was a glass tank. Smoky gas swirled around inside. On the bottom was a slot. An energy cell was fitted neatly inside.

It's just like the one Dwayne took from

the camera back at the White Pointer! Zac thought. His skin prickled with excitement. He was onto something!

Zac saw what was going on. The energy drained out of the cell and into the tank. Then the machine spat out a piece of paper.

```
        7:17 a.m.

   FINAL TEST PHASE

  UPLOAD SUCCESSFUL
```

Suddenly, Zac heard the sound of crying coming from the CCTV screens.

Zac looked closer and saw a red-headed woman selling tickets to very little kids in the White Pointer's ticket booth.

When Zac rode the White Pointer, he thought the ticket-seller was bending the rules to be nice. But now he saw what was really going on.

When they got to the front of the line, the little kids could see how scary the ride was. *But that woman's not letting them change their minds,* Zac thought angrily. *That's why they're in tears.*

He hit *Zoom* on the TV. A cold chill clutched him. The woman looked just like Dwayne! According to the GIB database, there was one woman who looked like Dwayne...

Former BIG star Janet Wolfe!

How can this be a BIG plot when neither of the enemy agents works for BIG? Zac wondered.

His brain was about to explode. He stared at the CCTV screen. Janet Wolfe's hair shone a brilliant red.

Sometimes redheads are nicknamed Ginger, Zac thought slowly. *Dwayne and Janet look alike. Maybe they're brother and sister. Ginger is Dwayne's pet name for Janet!*

Whoever they were, Ginger and Dwayne were purposely scaring the kids on the White Pointer.

I've got do something, Zac thought. He fished his grappling hook out of his backpack. The grappling hook was a sturdy hook on the end of a long rope.

Zac flung the hook into the air. It caught the edge of the trap door that he'd fallen through earlier.

Zac shimmied up the rope. He held onto the treasure chest to haul himself through the trap door. Seconds later, he was outside again.

What's the quickest way to the White Pointer? he asked himself. *I know — I'll just follow the screams.*

CHAPTER... EIGHT

Zac raced toward the White Pointer. Every shark-shaped carriage was filled with bawling kids.

Zac shoved his way through the line and onto the platform. But he was too late! The White Pointer and its terrified passengers were leaving the platform.

Legs coiled like springs, Zac launched

himself into the air. The White Pointer was gathering speed. Zac jumped through the air toward it. Would he make it?

Yes! He caught the last carriage and clung onto the shark's teeth.

With the safety cable built into his belt, Zac clipped himself to the carriage. He moved forward to the front carriage and squeezed in beside two bawling kids.

The White Pointer shot into a tight upside-down corkscrew. The passengers were screaming their lungs out!

"LISTEN UP!" yelled Zac, turning around so everyone could hear. "I'M GOING TO TEACH YOU THE ZAC POWER METHOD OF FEARLESSNESS!" he bellowed as the White Pointer flew into a loop-the-loop.

Er...what is that, exactly? Zac thought, racking his brains. *I'm never scared because I believe I don't get scared,* he thought. *So if I can make the kids believe they're not afraid, they won't be either!*

Zac remembered something from GIB's boring Fear Management course.

Concentrating on something else is a good way to stop feeling scared...

Zac had an idea. Maybe it was too simple to work, but it was worth a go!

"REPEAT AFTER ME!" Zac yelled to the kids. "SIX SHARP SMART SHARKS!"

"Six smarp smark…" the kids chorused.

The harder the kids tried to repeat Zac's tongue twister, the harder it was. Some of them started giggling, even though the ride was still going. "Six smart shark sharps," they said.

The kids were laughing so much they weren't even scared by the robotic White Pointer jumping out at them in the tunnel.

My silly tongue twister's actually working, thought Zac. *Unbelievable!*

Before the kids realized it, the ride had

finished. They streamed out of the carriages and ran straight to their parents.

Zac scanned the crowd. There was Ginger, her eyes glittering with rage. For a moment, their eyes locked. Then she started to run toward Zac.

She saw me help the kids, Zac realized, bolting. *I can't let her catch me! The mission isn't finished. Plus, she might use her Paralysis Grip on me!*

Zac's mind raced as fast as his legs. He had to work out what Ginger and Dwayne were up to. And he still needed to bug the conference centre.

His 24 hours were almost up!

Ginger was deliberately scaring kids on the

White Pointer. She got mad when I stopped the kids being afraid. And what about the Fear Factors I found at HQ?

Hang on...

Fear! Everything at Shark Park revolved around fear. *But where do the fake cameras and energy cells fit?* Zac wondered.

His breathing ragged, Zac checked over his shoulder. Every muscle burned. But Ginger was gaining on him! She ran like a machine, arms pumping, teeth gritted.

The thought of Ginger's Paralysis Grip gave Zac a burst of nervous energy.

Energy, Zac thought. *When I think of something scary, it creates energy!*

And then he worked it out. *The Wolfes are using fear as a form of energy! Terrified kids go on the White Pointer. Fear seeps out of the kids in waves. The cells hidden in the cameras collect and store the fear waves as energy.*

He heard footsteps close behind him. Ginger was close enough to grab him!

"Excuse me, madam, would you like a shark balloon?" said a man selling balloons. At the perfect moment, he had stepped in Ginger's way.

"MORON!" screeched Ginger, shoving the man out of the way.

But those few seconds were all Zac needed to slip from Ginger's grasp. He sped off, looking for a place to hide.

The Gummy Shark ride was nearby. A sign read:

UNDER CONSTRUCTION

Perfect, thought Zac. He opened the door of the Gummy Shark ride and crept in.

Inside the building, it was dark and empty.

What a scam! thought Zac. *They're not building a new ride here!*

Then a voice rang out of the darkness. "Ready, aim, FIRE!"

CHAPTER... ...NINE

Zac ducked. Was someone going to shoot him? There was a loud blast and a flash of light. In that split second, Zac saw who was yelling.

It was Dwayne Wolfe. He was holding a ray gun, squinting through the telescopic gunsight at a target on the opposite wall.

What is this place? Zac wondered. *Are*

the Wolfes using the Gummy Shark as a firing range? He pressed himself flat to the wall. *I definitely don't trust a dummy like Dwayne with a ray gun,* Zac thought.

There was another blast and a flash.

"I bet you've never seen a Fear-ray gun before!" Dwayne yelled.

He's talking to himself! thought Zac. *He's crazy.*

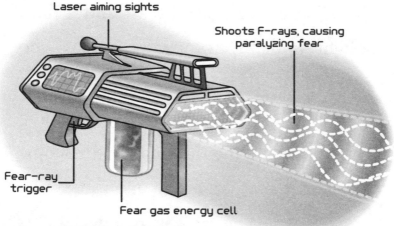

Laser aiming sights

Shoots F-rays, causing paralyzing fear

Fear-ray trigger

Fear gas energy cell

FEAR-RAY GUN

"There's only one in the world and it's ours! Who's smart now, you BIG losers?"

Fear-ray gun? thought Zac. *The gun must be shooting out fear!*

All of a sudden, Zac understood what the Wolfes were doing at Shark Park. A Fear-ray gun would need a constant supply of fear. Once Ginger left BIG, she would've had time to build a theme park. The money would fund her evil plans, and the park itself would help her carry them out.

But why's Dwayne talking about BIG? Zac thought. *He was never a BIG agent.*

Then Zac remembered Ginger telling Dwayne he would have made a great agent.

What a lie! Dwayne would be a terrible BIG agent. He wasn't smart. He was careless about covering his tracks. It was probably him who left the boxes at the garbage dump.

A theory formed in Zac's mind.

Maybe Dwayne tried out to be a BIG agent, he thought. *But he wasn't smart enough. Ginger was hurt that BIG thought her brother was dumb, so she resigned in protest.*

There was an obvious conclusion.

Ginger and Dwayne want revenge on BIG! They're planning to attack the conference with the Fear-ray gun!

Zac knew the Fear-ray gun wouldn't hurt the BIG agents. But it would seriously scare them. They'd be humiliated, just like BIG had humiliated Ginger and Dwayne.

Building a theme park and convincing BIG to hold its annual conference there seemed like a lot of effort to Zac. But he guessed that Ginger hadn't reached the top of the evil spy world by thinking small.

Anyway, what did it matter to Zac if the BIG agents were scared? The most important thing was to stop Ginger and Dwayne escaping with the Fear-ray gun.

But a tickle was rising in Zac's nose. It was so dusty in the Gummy Shark!

The tickle grew, until…

"ACHOO!" Zac sneezed loudly.

"Hey," Dwayne yelled in the dark. "Is someone there?"

Well, duh, thought Zac, bolting for the door. But then…

A blast! A flash of light! An ice-cold quiver shot through Zac's body. Dwayne had shot him with the Fear-ray gun.

"Ginger!" Dwayne shouted into his walkie-talkie. "An intruder!"

Zac tried to speak. But no words came out. Zac's bottom lip was trembling too hard.

If I don't run, Ginger's going to catch me, Zac thought, frightened. But he couldn't run. The fear was too strong. Zac was so scared, he couldn't move.

I'm worse than the kids on the White Pointer.

Then he had an idea. "*Six sharp smart sharks!*" he whispered. He tried to say it faster. "*Six shark smarp…*" he said. Zac stopped. "No, that's wrong. It's *sax smarp…*"

Zac grinned. The fear drained out of him. The ridiculous tongue twister had worked again.

"Dwayne Wolfe," Zac yelled. "I'm Zac Power, GIB. Hand over that Fear-ray gun immediately!"

Dwayne scratched his head, surprised. He wasn't quite sure what to do.

A smarter person would just shoot me with the Fear-ray again, thought Zac.

Moments later, Dwayne had the same idea. He blasted the fear at Zac — twice!

But while Dwayne was hesitating, Zac had taken off his backpack and held it in front of him like a shield.

KER-RACK!

Zac's iPod was stashed in the front pocket of his backpack. The fear smashed into it. There was a shower of sparks bigger than the finale of an Axe Grinder concert.

The force shot Zac backwards. His iPod was a black, smoking ruin! But the plan worked. The double dose of fear went bouncing back at Dwayne.

Dwayne's eyes went saucer-wide. "I WANT MY MUMMY!" he bawled loudly, snot dripping from his nose.

Zac raced over to Dwayne. He

snatched the Fear-ray and stuffed it in his backpack.

That's the gun taken care of, thought Zac. *Guess I can go and bug the BIG conference centre now. There's just enough time.*

"Not so fast," said a voice behind him. It was Ginger!

CHAPTER... ...TEN

"You've got the Fear-ray, Power," snarled Ginger. "And you've foiled our revenge on BIG."

She grabbed the terrified Dwayne by the hand. She slapped him across the cheek, shocking him out of his fear.

"But you'll never outfox the Wolfes!" she yelled.

She and Dwayne raced out of the Gummy Shark building. Zac raced after them. He couldn't let the Wolfes escape!

But as Zac knew, Ginger was a very fast runner. She and Dwayne had shot ahead.

Looks like they're heading for the World of Sharks! Zac thought.

Zac burst through the doors into the World of Sharks aquarium. But where were Ginger and Dwayne?

Then he heard something.

R-RR-RRRRRRR!

A pair of engines, revving loudly. Zac scanned the room. The sub shark tank! For some reason, the water was churning like crazy. Jerry cans of gasoline littered the floor. And the Wolfes had disappeared.

The clues added up to one thing. *Sub sharks aren't real sharks!* Zac realized. *They're submarines disguised as sharks! The tank is connected to the open sea, so the Sub Sharks are perfect for emergency escapes.*

Zac filled his lungs with air and then

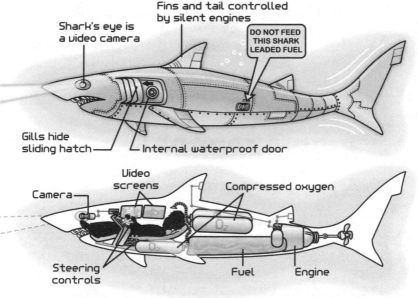

SUB SHARK Personal Stealth Submarine

leaped into the tank. *I really, really hope my theory's right!* thought Zac, grabbing the nearest Sub Shark round the middle.

Phew! Zac thought. The shark was made of metal. And where the gills should have been, Zac found a hatch.

Zac popped the hatch open. He slid inside the Sub Shark's body. There was just enough room to lie flat on his back. An oxygen tank piped in fresh air.

Through the Sub Shark's eyes, Zac spotted a pipe at the bottom of the tank. *The exit to the sea!* he thought, pressing a button that said *Escape* and diving downward.

With its powerful metal fins, the sub sliced through the water like a blade.

I've always loved sharks, thought Zac. *Now I know how it feels to swim like one!*

On the sub's instrument panel, a radar screen blipped. Two shark-shaped blobs were speeding away from Shark Park. The Wolfes!

Zac shot after them. A school of silvery fish nibbled at a cloud of seaweed just ahead. Zac blasted straight through the school. Fish scattered in every direction.

They're terrified! Zac thought. *Causing fear is a powerful feeling. Dangerously powerful...*

If not for Zac taking the Fear-ray gun, the Wolfes would have had that power any time they wanted.

Gotta get them, Zac thought, shifting the

sub into overdrive. Then all of a sudden the blobs on the radar disappeared.

He'd lost Dwayne and Ginger! Dwayne might be thick, but Ginger had proven again that she knew how to disappear.

Reluctantly, Zac turned the Sub Shark around and headed back. After climbing out of the Sub Shark, Zac trudged toward the conference centre. He checked the time.

Forty-seven minutes to place the bugs, he thought.

But when Zac reached the conference centre, it was deserted. A notice was pinned to the door.

TODAY'S CONFERENCE CANCELLED DUE TO UNFORESEEN CIRCUMSTANCES

BIG intelligence must have already been onto Dwayne and Ginger!

This was a super annoying way to end a mission! *The Wolfes got away. It looks like there's no conference. Guess I won't be making the top of the Spy Ladder again this week.*

Although it does mean I'll have time to ride the White Pointer again...

Then Zac's SpyPad rang.

"Agent Clawhammer here, how's everything going?"

"Remember Janet Wolfe?" Zac began. "She invented a Fear-ray gun that I now have —"

"Debrief us when you return," Clawhammer said. "Agent Bumsmack, a.k.a Mum, orders Agent Rock Star home immediately via high-speed jet. You're expected at Angus's party."

Nooooo! An afternoon playing musical chairs with a bunch of kids, sighed Zac. *And I thought spying was tough...*

... THE END ...

POISON ISLAND 1

DEEP WATERS 2

MIND GAMES 3

FROZEN FEAR 4

TOMB OF DOOM 5

NIGHT RAID 6

LUNAR STRIKE 7

SUDDEN DROP 8

BLOCKBUSTER 9

SHOCKWAVE 10

HIGH RISK 11

UNDERCOVER 12

SKY HIGH 13

VOLCANIC PANIC 14

BOOT CAMP 15

SWAMP RACE 16

HORROR HOUSE 17

THRILL RIDE 18